SALAD DAYS

Enakshi J.

Published by InkQuills Publishing House

www.inkquills.in

First Edition 2024

All Rights Reserved. Copyright © 2024

ISBN: 978-93-90567-76-8

*To the wanderers and wonderers, may these words
guide you through the uncharted territories of your own
thoughts and dreams.*

Introduction

Love, that beguiling muse, has woven a tapestry of emotions throughout the annals of time, a tapestry that is often as twisted as the Gordian knot itself. To navigate the labyrinth of love is to embark on a journey where the heart, that fickle compass, guides one through both the sublime and the shadowy realms. As Shakespeare aptly proclaimed, "The course of true love never did run smooth," and indeed, the path of love is fraught with unexpected twists and turns.

Someone once asked me if I had experienced Generation Gap. My answer was an obvious yes but what surprised me was the example that I quoted; I spoke about how I was too different from the others of my age. While my generation thrived on cafes and all-night calls, I dreamt of old-school love letters. Texting was experiencing a revolution of its own, lovers made promises of eternity by exhausting their fingers relentlessly. However, my unrelenting urge to follow the rules of the language made me an oddball. And then, in the blink of an eye, the definition of love changed too.

Nostalgia is harsh at times. And the lingering fragrance of outmoded affection is something to die for!

Hence, as a coping mechanism, I used my imagination to breathe life into several such characters who were characterized by traditional values, chivalry, and a slower, more deliberate pace. Their stories involve handwritten letters, courtship rituals, and a commitment to long-term relationships. Respect, loyalty, and a strong sense of partnership are central to this old-school love, and gestures like flowers, door-opening, and face-to-face communication are important. As cliched as it might sound, this is my haven after all.

In the realm of love, one often encounters the deceptive allure of Cupid's arrow, a weapon that can transform the most rational minds into ardent fools. Bard had once remarked, "Love looks not with the eyes, but with the mind." Love defies logic and reason in its twisted complexity, leaving one trapped in a web of passion and desire. It is a force that blinds, entangles, and confounds, turning the most prudent souls into unwitting participants in a romantic masquerade.

The idiom "love is blind" finds its resonance in the profound truth that love can obscure reality, veiling flaws and imperfections in a cloak of infatuation. Like a spell cast upon the unsuspecting, the twisted nature of love often blinds individuals to the shortcomings of their beloved. In the throes of passion, one may willingly overlook the proverbial "red flags," choosing instead to dance on the precipice of blissful ignorance. Hence, giving the necessary spotlight that my mind deserves, the stories in this collection are not the ones that promise a happily-ever-after but they're more pragmatic, sometimes, even overwhelming. But true at the core.

Delving into the enchanting realm of love stories possesses a unique virtue, as it orchestrates a symphony of emotions that resonates deeply within the chambers of one's heart. The intricacies of characters navigating the delicate dance of affection bestow upon the reader a tapestry of sentiments, nurturing a profound sense of empathy. Such literary dalliances elevate the soul, crafting a mosaic of emotional intelligence that gracefully transcends the boundaries of fiction into the fabric of reality. This ballet of emotions not only captivates the imagination but also, akin to a fragrant zephyr, gently caresses the heart, fostering an ethereal connection that renders one's relational landscape more vibrant and resilient. In this elegant ballet, the heart finds solace and elevation, affirming the notion that the pursuit of love, even in the written word, is a sublime tonic for the soul.

Salad Days, one of Shakespeare's idioms, refers to the period when one is young and inexperienced (Oxford Dictionary). For those of you who have read my work before, it might not come as a surprise that I'm obsessed with Shakespeare's idioms and my books are titled using those play-on-words. Hence, Salad Days aims to take you all on a heartfelt journey about love, loss, fateful encounters, star-crossed lovers and unrequited love. In this collection of short stories, get ready to immerse yourselves in nostalgia, mushy romance and unanticipated heartaches.

Salad Days is an earnest attempt to explain one and all that love is intangible. It's irresistible too. Sometimes blissful, sometimes compulsion, but often associated with a blinding sweet effect. It comes unannounced and leaves before warning. When you want it not, it decides to visit you and urges you to reconsider all your pragmatic decisions!

In conclusion, the tapestry of love is a rich and intricate weave, adorned with the threads of passion, betrayal, jealousy, and unrequited affection. Shakespeare, that unparalleled maestro of the human heart, has provided us with a mirror to reflect upon the twisted nature of love. From the poetic heights of "A Midsummer Night's Dream" to the tragic depths of "Romeo and Juliet" and "Othello," love's kaleidoscopic hues have been explored with unparalleled eloquence. As we navigate the labyrinthine path of love, let us heed the wisdom of the Bard and recognize that, in love's twisted complexity, the heart is both a compass and a tempest, guiding us through the tumultuous seas of passion and desire.

Credits:

The Whimsical Flautist was first published in Woman's Era.

Contents

A Silver Lining to Burnt Toast

Some moons ago if someone had told me that my wedding would be a lavish affair, I would have let out a giant belly laugh. But there I was that day waiting eagerly to get married to the man whom I adored and cherished. Adorned with church doors, the entrance to the venue was exquisite. Ribbons, flowers, miniature maple plants and cylindrical accordion paper lanterns formed a canopy of vibrant colours. As I moved a little further, hundreds of rainbow-like umbrellas floated over the aisle. Two huge palm leaves on either side of the mandap waited eagerly for the bride and the groom. Zayn stood on the other end with that sly 'come hither' stare. His eyes spoke volumes. Dressed to the nines, he was the most fanciable man in the gathering. I was lucky!

Zayn and I had met in college. Poles apart as far as our interests were considered, we still connected well when it came to opinionated discussions. I met him through a common friend, Adah. She was Zayn's neighbour. An atheist by nature, Zayn was pragmatic yet often succumbed to emotions. His inability to forget and move on often got the better of him. Maybe that was the reason why he treasured solitude more than anything. Even more than me! The decision to marry him was not rushed because I took a good three years to understand the difference between infatuation and love. But the aftermath of the decision was something that left us marked for life.

Zayn's parents were not in favour of our alliance. His mother would bring up the topic of religious differences, my incapability to fit in and she would easily get away with those biased and racist comments.

My parents were no different. The moment my house would become eerie quiet and only whispers could be heard; I could make out that my parents were fomenting trouble. My father was still a patient man. But my mother let all hell break loose when I told her about Zayn.

"Have you lost your mind? He is a Baniya," she chastised.

"I know that. How does it matter? He is a good human being and he is loyal. What more do you want?" I claimed.

"God gave you a brain, didn't he? Why don't you use it? Your actions will have serious consequences," she restated.

"Yes, I know that my actions will have a consequence- that I will be happy. Why is it such a big deal?"

I had already anticipated the next step. My father kept his cup of tea on the table with a loud bang, looked at my mother with anger and left the dining area.

Let's play the quiet game- I thought. Knowing that convincing my parents wasn't an easy cookie to crack, threw my hands up in exasperation and asked my mother for the one last time (or so I thought), "Will you please listen to me first before passing your judgement?"

She didn't respond. Gathering the pleats of her cotton sari, she got up from the sofa and marched towards the kitchen. There was no point in carrying on with the argument. I let my parents be, for anything that I would have said at that moment, wouldn't have made any difference.

I went back to my college after surviving the most dreaded weekend of my life. Disappointed at my parents' beliefs, I tried several times to decipher the logic behind the caste system and the prejudices against the people of different castes but I failed miserably. Zayn and I were educated. Still, we had to be a part of the battle of wills where logic and reasoning didn't exist. It took two years of convincing and coaxing for our parents to agree to grant us moments of nuptial bliss. However, our happiness was a nine-day wonder. The eagerly anticipated visitors — typical stereotypes — soon arrived and began setting the stage for chaos in our lives.

The wedding preparations were supposed to be minimal because both Zayn and I were penny pinchers. We thought of getting married in a temple that would be followed by a small reception. But alas! Only if our troubles ceased there! My mother, a typical ostentatious Punjabi woman that she was, refused to listen to us. She wanted the wedding to be her way or the highway! Consequently, Goa's most lavish resort near the beachside was booked. I couldn't argue because I was well aware of the fact that he who pays the piper, calls the tunes.

As long as our parents didn't sit together to finalize things, it was smooth. But a day before the Henna Ceremony, when all my aunts and uncles, along with other armchair critics, sat down in the dining area to discuss the functions in detail, all pandemonium broke loose.

My mother's sister asked me, "Nitya, you could have found someone far better than Zain- someone whose name was easier to pronounce- someone who belonged to the same caste. Why Zain then?"

"His name is Zayn, not Zain. Aunty, I think you should join 'Mind Cultivation' classes because as far as I remember, you were the one who always taught us that there is no caste in blood. These toxic thoughts won't get you anywhere," I pointed out.

"Shut up, Nitya," my mother chided, a frown of frustration evident on her forehead.

"What the point of shutting her up now, Lata? The damage has already been done," ranted another uncle of mine.

My mother gave me a stare that sent shivers down my spine. I knew what was in store for me. And thus, I kept quiet. A few moments later, when the guests realised that they had been talking to a brick wall, the conversation changed course. Now, it was about the Big Fat Punjabi Wedding.

I had tried several times to argue the toss and convince my mother not to spend so lavishly on my wedding. But she had her own reasons, reasons that were ostensibly backed by the beliefs of the conformists.

"We have to show them how a Punjabi wedding is organized. They should see our status and understand that we are one of the most elite people in the society," she would articulate often.

"Is there a competition between you and Zayn's mother? Why do you need to prove anything?" I would ask.

"You don't understand. This is how society works. If you do not show people their rightful place, they can drive you up the wall."

"That's not the right reason. You are simply making a mountain out of a mole. Zayn's parents didn't say a word about the wedding arrangements, did they?" I enquired.

"You are at your wit's end. You aren't thinking straight. What will people say when they see your name with Zayn's? They will question his religion. They will question the fact that you both are of the same age. They will question our decision to agree to your marriage," she faltered.

"But Ma, Zayn is a mature individual. He is not only practical but also nice. I am sure he will not let you down. Don't you think it is better for me to marry someone I know rather than marrying someone I don't?"

"How do you think your father and I got married? We were not in love. We fell in love after marriage and that is how it is supposed to happen. All this wouldn't have happened if you had listened to me and got married to Aryan, Mrs Kapoor's son, who lives in Canada. You kept on postponing the decision and see now- you are 30!" My mother's voice was stern and resolute.

"Aryan has nothing to do with all this. Just because he is a Punjabi doesn't mean that he is a good man as well.

How can you be so naive to measure goodness in terms of caste and money?"

She stomped on the floor and left the room with flared nostrils.

The scenario in Zayn's house was no different. His parents criticized his decision to choose a Punjabi girl. According to them, my extravagant nature wouldn't match with their son's nature. Ever. However hard he tried; they turned a deaf ear to all his pleas. The unspoken war enraged our relatives as well. Knowing that we all are the same at the emotional level, I couldn't quite understand the reason for this disparity. It is not possible to understand everything at once. We cannot begin with perfection at once. Where having an open mind was the need of the hour, there I was- stuck in a debate that aimed at proving that my caste was more respectable than Zayn's. I knew that our parents needed time. But I never expected them to be so vocal about their feelings. They didn't care if their words hurt anyone and that eventually, paved the path for the relatives.

On the D Day, after the traditional rituals had been successfully carried out, Adah was asked to raise a toast in our honour. She, being our common friend, knew us inside out. Surprisingly, she politely refused the invitation, saying she would like to conclude the function with her toast.

"I would like to raise a toast to the newly married couple," shouted Zayn's uncle (in an attempt to jeer at us).

Zayn gestured to his sister to hush his uncle but to no avail. He had already taken the reigns of the function in his hands by then.

"Dear Nitya and Zayn,

It is such a good day to share my feelings as both families are together. I am happy today-not because Zayn decided to marry against our will. I am happy because I had a good time drinking beer and lazying around on the beach. Well, we all have had enough stress to deal with already and now is the time to rejoice. But still, I would say that I would never allow my children to consult Zayn in matters of love. Nitya, Baniyas are very accommodating people but we will have to see about the Punjabis…" he snickered but was cut short by my aunt the very next moment.

"Look at that- all hat and no cattle! Punjabis are known for their large heart and benevolence. Zayn is lucky to have found Nitya. She will take good care of him." she finished.

"Really? I think you should be grateful that Zayn decided to marry your daughter, for she wouldn't have got any luckier than this owing to her vociferous nature!" Zayn's other aunt retorted.

"Look who's talking. You should first learn to decide the right name for your son. What kind of name is Zayn? Are his parents Muslims that you have kept such a name?" responded my uncle in my defence.

The word battle went on for another fifteen-twenty minutes and the time moved at the pace of a snail. Both Zayn and I were left rooted to the spot. We couldn't fathom the hypocrisy of our families. They didn't care about society anymore because they forgot that they were a part of one! They didn't care if we were happy. In the constant struggle to prove one's worth, they stooped down so low that even the society started to seem better!

"And with this, we come to my turn," interrupted Adah.

I didn't know what was in store for us. The smile of exhilaration that once adorned our lips had been replaced with a crestfallen look.

"Dear Zayn and Nitya,

It is your big day and I wouldn't miss this opportunity to tell you both how much I love you. I had been waiting for this day for a long time. When Zayn first asked me about Nitya, I knew something was up! Love brewed between them and they forgot that they ever had friends. Or so we thought. Cutting to the chase, it wouldn't be right to say that they don't value us. In fact, I think they value us more than their family members. I wish both of them luck, love and luxury in the years to come. They are both mature and understanding. But I haven't finished my toast yet. This part of my speech is completely dedicated to Zayn's and Nitya's relatives.

Knowing that our brain is hardwired to pass judgements at the drop of a hat, it isn't wrong to reach a conjecture. But voicing out your opinion in public and engaging in a squabble only shows how immature you are. Fighting on the basis of someone's financial status, gender or caste is inconsequential. The entire conversation that you all had was so stereotypical. I do realize that falling prey to certain stereotypes is common but then allowing those stereotypes to go beyond that impulse and hamper someone's judgement is pathetic. Do you all still call yourselves grown-ups? You all always taught us to be impartial and non-judgemental. But are you practising what you preach? I know this is going to hurt but the truth is that your words were equivalent to a thousand pins piercing on the same wound. I am sorry Nitya and Zayn on behalf of all our elders." Adah finished, thereby inviting judgemental glares and scornful expressions.

"Seema, see how your daughter's friend insulted us?" poked my aunt.

It is best to leave out what followed next. We realized that friends are like lifelines. They are like the buoy in the ocean consisting of crests and troughs. We hold onto them as their positive energy enables us to sail forth combating all the troubles that lie ahead. Adah had saved our day, at least for us! The way our relatives were hurling insults at each other, it seemed as if the battle would go on forever and both Zayn and I would be trapped in this whirlpool of taunts forever. But Adah understood that a silver lining in that burnt toast was exactly what was needed to set the wheels of our love story rolling.

Blind Luck

Running like a half-wit person, sweating under the fierce glare of the afternoon sun, I looked left and then right and finally came to a halt. My breathing could be heard so loud that it could put a stethoscope to shame. Delirious because of the afternoon heat, I decided to give up the search. As soon as I turned to head back to the bookstore, I collided and fell flat on the ground. Unable to feel my hands, I thought I had died. A gentle spray of water helped me regain my consciousness.

"Are you alright?" asked a male voice.

"I guess," I stammered.

Squinting my eyes to recognize the face of the person standing before me, I tried to get up. Aching limbs and bruised palms didn't quite let me up though. He helped me get up and then asked, "Do I dazzle you?"

"What?" I asked.

"You didn't understand, did you?"

"No, I didn't," I said, agitated at the irrelevant conversation that was taking away my energy.

He didn't explain any further. It did not take rocket science for me to connect the dots and understand what he was trying to say. He was the same man whom I was chasing or rather searching for. He was the one with whom I had participated in the 'Book-o-holics-Carry on the Conversation' competition. He was too good at it. And I had made a run for him after the event was over because I wanted to return his copy of 'Postscript'.

A few hours before

Bored and jobless on a weekday, I decided to go to Crossword and check out the new books. I had taken a day off as my client, too, was on leave and I didn't have much to do without him. Being a lawyer came with its boons and woes! What better occasion than this to take a day off? As I packed a few essentials into my sling bag, my dog, Silver, jumped on me and pushed me hard on the sofa. Silver ruined my yellow dress and made me change into a pastel blue coloured t-shirt. Why these details are important, you might ask? Well, it was this blue T-shirt that made me get selected for the competition.

That's the thing about Crossword. They are so dynamic. They keep on organizing such promotional events and the reviewers and the bloggers can get the best out of such competitions. 'Book-o-holics-Carry on the Conversation' was one such competition. Each participant was randomly paired with another and they had to prove their knowledge of the books by first identifying the speaker (character) and then completing the dialogue. The selectors just announced 'All blues pair together' and there it went. With no blue shirt in sight, I felt dejected. But just then someone spoke, "This is the door to both sustenance and sanity. And we are each other's key."

I couldn't help but pass a smile. He was a Hunger Games fan and I knew it that very instant that our pair would easily win this competition.

"Hi, I am Purab. I don't think anyone else is in blue so you will have to bear with me while I poke my brain cells to win this game." He finished in one breath.

"Hi, I am Preeshi. I don't mind bearing the brunt of your actions as long as the brunt is sweet!" I tried to sound smarter.

"Our names alliterate! Such a positive coincidence." He concluded.

He extended his hand, inviting me to join him as we made our way to the main stage where the book enthusiasts had already gathered.

After a series of dialogues to complete, we waited with bated breath for the last set. The moderator handed Purab a chit. Already a bundle of nerves, I stared at him, waiting for him to deliver his line. I only had 10 seconds to identify the character whose line he would be delivering and another 20 to complete the conversation.

"My family, we're different from others of our kind. We only hunt animals. We've learned to control our thirst but it's you, your scent, it's like a drug to me. You're like you're my own personal brand of heroin," said Purab and waited.

My mind was in jitters. I knew this line so well that I had forgotten the source! Purab had started getting heebie-jeebies by then.

"Why did you hate me so much when we met?" I asked.

"I did, only because of wanting you so badly. I still don't know if I can control myself." He muttered.

"I know you can," I comforted.

"Yes, we know you both can and you have done it. Congratulations on winning this competition," shouted the moderator.

Overwhelmed with joy, Purab and I hugged each other but the invisible societal bounds made us realize quickly the repercussions of our actions. We chatted for a little while before parting ways. I got to know that he was an avid reader and worked in an IT company.

Fast forward a few hours and there we were on the street, facing each other again.

"What is my book doing in your bag?" He questioned.

"You had dropped it in the store. So, I was running behind you to return it."

"Did you open it or read it?"

"Why would I do that? How is it relevant? Are you out of your mind?" I rebuked.

"Preeshi, how can you not open a book when you find it!"

I didn't understand what he meant. It is only when my roommate suggested that he might have left his phone number in the book that I had my light bulb moment. But it was too late, wasn't it?

Days passed in a jiffy and I couldn't even spend one moment not thinking about him. His dishevelled teased platinum hair, ramrod straight and rock-jawed, with gunmetal eyes and shoulders that seemed mitred at a perfect ninety-degree angle- all of these kept flashing before my eyes. Was I in love? I couldn't possibly be as I had only met him once. That was impractical. I tried to brush aside these thoughts before they took over my thinking ability.

"Preeshi, come down for breakfast," shouted Amita, my roommate.

"Coming in five," I shouted back.

"There is someone to meet you. Scurry downstairs, now!" Amita chided.

Who would have come to meet me on a Sunday, I wondered. As I paced down the stairs, I realized that I looked as ugly as a duckling. With my hair all over my face, my kohl spread like butter on my cheeks and my tousled head, I was sure to scare away the visitor.

"You? What are you doing here? How did you know that I lived here?" I shot an array of questions.

Purab's mystified look made me curse my folly. While on one hand, I wished to see him so desperately, I didn't even think twice before shooting so many questions at him.

"Calm down, Preeshi. I just read the book that you left for me on the road."

"Book? Which book? When did I leave any book?' I tried pretending.

"Really? You might not be eager to read the notes left behind in someone else's book but I am. I found your address in 'Every Breath' that you left on the road. You had bookmarked the page with the bill! Who does that?" He shot a disgusted look.

"I do that. What's wrong with that? At least you got to know my address, didn't you?"

"Yes, I did. Now make my effort worthwhile by agreeing to come for a coffee with me," he grinned.

Smiling faintly, I gestured to Amita that I would be having breakfast outside. Rushing upstairs to do a slight touch-up, I asked Purab to sit and read for a while. What followed next was a series of outings where two Literature enthusiasts shared optimism, memorable dialogues and delved deeper into the world of love where twilight brought hope, letters brought back memories and bottles carried messages of love.

Rendezvous with Happenstance

Heat licked our sunburned faces as we walked out of the fifth shop. The torridity coiled around our limbs like a hot-blooded serpent. Shopping had become the bane of our lives. However, it was important; only a few days were left for the parade. Missy's mother wanted her to buy a nice set of ethnic wear from the lavish shops of Chandni Chawk in Delhi. Moreover, who could be a better ally than me? After all, Missy and I had been soul sisters for a long time- right from when we started school until we landed our first job (in the same company). Even though Missy wasn't interested in getting married, the idea of dressing up ostentatiously and dancing around in front of a strange family appeased her. She was always a brandish! I was the opposite. This concept of objectifying women in order to find them a nice suitor drove me up the wall. Alas! Friendship- a sweet responsibility that I had to fulfill!

It required us three days to settle on the Mauve-colored kurta featuring an embroidered lotus at the centre paired with contrasting leggings. Despite the hefty price tag, Missy appeared discontented with her selection. Goodness! If I were in her position, I would have felt grateful for the chance to purchase such an extravagant outfit. The next task on our agenda was finding matching jewellery, but that's a tale for another time.

The D-Day arrived soon and as I made my way into her superfluously decorated house, I realised that I wasn't quite dressed to the nines. Feeling a little out of place, I decided to trace back my steps, go back to my house and change. No sooner had I turned back than I collided with Missy's aunt who had come all the way from Jalandhar.

"Greetings, Aunt Hema! How are you?" I responded.

"Bless you, my child! How are you? See how much you have grown- in both height and weight- I must say. So, when are your wedding bells going to ring?" she exulted.

"In two months. Didn't you get the invite?" I taunted.

"No, I didn't. Who is the groom? I hope he has a six-figure salary." She retorted.

I had read an article somewhere on 'Seven nasty replies for the ladies who ask you about your marriage' and that day I realised that such articles are a hoax. I looked at my watch and slurred.

"Hema aunty, I have to get going. Missy asked me to get her jewellery box which she left in my house."

"How is this possible? Missy showed me her entire set of ornaments this morning! How can she..." She looked perplexed.

"No, not those. I have her other jewellery sets." I interjected and wished for the aunt's quick departure to hell.

Before she could rip my confidence apart with her sharp words again, her attention was drawn to the lady who just entered the huge black gate.

"Who is she?" she asked no one in particular.

"Let's go find out," I deflected.

We walked together for a few seconds and then I took a different course. She was more bothered about that lady than being worried about where I was going. As I tried to pull the latch of the back gate of Missy's house, the metal bar flung at me. Miraculously, it did not hit me. Soon enough I realized that it wasn't God's doing. Sarthak, my classmate from school had saved me. Wondering how he ended up there, I shot an array of questions.

"Sarthak, how come you are here?"

"You're welcome," he snapped.

I hated him. We were the rival competitors in school. Even half a mark mattered a lot between us. Both of us being toppers, we always had a reason to fight. All those thoughts were suddenly brushed aside when I realized that he had not answered my question.

"Yes, that too. How come you are here?"

"You don't seem to like my presence, do you?"

"No, not really. How much will you charge for answering my question directly?" I continued.

"I have come to see Missy."

"But this isn't the right time. Her suitor will be here any moment. Why don't you come another day?"

"Well, unfortunately for you, I am her prospective groom." He chuckled.

His words blew the gasket. How could he become a member of our family (or the so-called family)?

"You should leave before somebody drops a house on you."

"What's your problem, Mirabai? While others drank from the fountain of knowledge, I think you just gargled."

"Really? And you were the lone child sitting beside the fountain wondering whether to get up or not!"

Before we could conclude our bickering, Missy came running towards us and pulled me aside.

"What are you doing, Mira? He is the groom."

"Have you lost your mind, Missy? Sarthak, of all the fools out there?"

"I didn't choose him. My parents did and I had no reason to object." She smiled coyly.

I couldn't argue the toss. Considering that Missy's parents were stereotypical, it would not be wrong to say that they had found the right groom for her. Sarthak, even though he was raw and sardonic, was intelligent and well-placed.

"I am not as stupid as you look. But I would say that this colour suits you." Sarthak chimed in.

"Really? Do you still want to continue?"

"Continue what?"

"I don't have the time or the crayons to explain this to you." I snapped and left from there.

The following hours were a test of endurance. I found myself confined to Missy's room, enduring her endless chatter about Sarthak's virtues and how her life would be a fairytale once she tied the knot with him. Like a saint in a storm, I clung to my patience, nodding along as if my life depended on it. Seeing my friend happy was my only solace.

The elders played their roles, engaging in their ritualistic decision-making, and promised to reconvene with their final verdict.

Two weeks dragged by before I received a distress call from Missy. She sobbed into the phone, recounting how her parents had reneged on the marriage proposal because her Aunt Hema had unearthed a superior suitor (probably with a six-figure salary, no doubt!) and insisted Missy accept this new alliance.

Ah, the wonders of family politics! It's like watching a soap opera scripted by chaos and directed by absurdity.

"Why don't you tell her that you like Sarthak?" I asked.

"Oh, Sarthak is the least of my worries. I'm bawling my eyes out because mother won't let me splurge on new parade attire. How am I supposed to strut in the same old outfit?" Missy lamented.

"Ah, yes, of course! How could I overlook such a monumental crisis!" I exclaimed dramatically, throwing my hands up in mock despair. The thud of my phone hitting the carpet snapped me out of my daze.

"Fret not, I shall venture forth and attempt to reason with your dear mother," I reassured her.

"Truly, Mira? You're a lifesaver!" Missy gushed.

Ah, the trials and tribulations of parade fashion! It's like navigating a minefield in stilettos.

She called me again after five minutes and what she said next put me between the devil and deep blue sea.

"I forgot to tell you one more thing. My parents told Sarthak that I refused for this marriage and when Sarthak called me to ask the reason, I didn't give him a clear reply. So, I told him that you will tell him the reason."

"What on earth was going in your mind, Missy? What am I to tell him? And why me?" I hollered.

"Because I know you will come up with something. Please help me out, Mira. Last time, I promise." She started sobbing again.

"Okay. I will think of something. You sleep."

I waited with a bated breath for a week for Sarthak's call. But my phone didn't buzz with his name on it.

Two weeks later

Ah, the joys of being chained to my laptop at my content curator's desk! My eyes were on the verge of mutiny, having gone through two pairs of glasses in just a month. Despite my dear mother's insistence on the miraculous powers of soaked raisins, my vision remained stubbornly blurry. Life was turning into a one-way ticket to Stressville, and I longed for a teleportation device to whisk me away to a land of peace and solitude. They say "Be careful what you wish for," and now I know why!

As Lalita, my trusty colleague, graciously offered me a cup of coffee, my phone erupted into a cacophony of buzzes, much to her surprise. With zero enthusiasm to entertain calls from unknown numbers, I hesitated, but curiosity got the better of me. Lo and behold, it was Missy calling from Dalhousie.

"Mira, guess what? Our old classmate, Manasvi, is tying the knot here in Dalhousie!" Missy exclaimed in one breath. "I asked her about inviting you, but I have a feeling she won't, given the fracas between you two. But fear not, I have a plan! Why don't you come over? We can explore the city together after the wedding."

"Sounds great, but what about my leaves? I can't conjure them out of thin air," I lamented.

"Oh, don't fret about that. I've got it all figured out," Missy reassured me with the confidence of a seasoned schemer. "It's Thursday today. Tomorrow, you work half a day and then conveniently 'fall ill' to leave the office early. Hop on a bus straight to Dalhousie. We'll have all of Saturday to gallivant around before heading back Sunday evening."

"And when's the wedding?" I inquired.

"Don't bother, it's happening as we speak!" Missy chirped.

Ah, Missy and her impulsive escapades! But truth be told, I was in desperate need of a break, so I agreed and followed her harebrained scheme to the letter. Little did I know what awaited me.

That evening, while Missy snored away like a contented elephant, I found myself rudely awakened by her incessantly ringing phone. Despite her blissful slumber, I rose to investigate, only to be met with the horror of seeing Sarthak's name illuminating the screen. Quickly silencing the device, I returned to bed, my mind reeling.

Minutes later, my own phone jolted me from my thoughts. With trepidation, I answered.

"Um, who's this?" I stammered.

"Well, don't you recognize my voice?" came the whispered response.

"What do you want?" I snapped, caught off guard.

"I knew you'd have my number. After all, you owe me an explanation," he teased, his words a jab at my vulnerability.

"What explanation? I have no desire to speak with you," I retorted sharply.

"I want to know why Missy turned me down. Was it because you see me as your future husband?" he jested, his tone mocking.

"What nonsense! Missy refused because you're simply not worth her time," I shot back.

Silence followed. Guilt pricked at my conscience. Had I been too harsh? Was he genuinely hurt? Why was I even caring? Clearing his throat, he interrupted my thoughts.

"Still there, Mirabai?" he inquired softly.

"Yes," I muttered.

"You sound down. Feeling guilty for being rude?" he probed.

"Um... no. Why would I—" I began, only to be cut off.

"Enough. Come outside, let's take a walk," he insisted.

"Wait... are you outside? How is that even possible?" I sputtered.

"Come out before I freeze," he urged, his voice coaxing me out into the chilly night.

Despite my resistance, his gentle persuasion won me over. Draping a shawl over my shoulders and slipping on my shoes, I tiptoed out, leaving the light on as I ventured into the darkness.

"I know why Missy said no," he started as we strolled through the night.

"Why's that?" I asked, curiosity piqued.

"Her family probably found a 'better' match," he quipped.

"I don't know about 'better,' but definitely 'richer'," I fired back, unable to resist the jab.

"Now where's your stress? All gone now that you've had the chance to mock someone 'better' than you?" he teased.

"Excuse me, 'better'? You were always a grumpy old man crying over everything — one mark less, one rank less, or one suitor less!" I retorted, my words laced with sarcasm.

Grinning in the darkness, he simply bowed his head and continued our walk. I squirmed uncomfortably, scolding myself for being so harsh.

"How did you end up in Dalhousie?" I finally asked, breaking the silence.

"I'm here with friends. Saw Missy at the bus stand yesterday and decided to drop by your place for answers," he explained.

"I'm sorry. Missy shouldn't have done this to you. But knowing her, it's hardly surprising," I conceded.

We spent another hour reminiscing in the nearby park, delving into memories of our competitive school days. We were the cream of the crop, vying for the top spots academically and athletically. He excelled in football, while I dominated the basketball court. Our camaraderie was unmatched, our rivalry fierce but friendly. The teachers even spared us from the headache of electing a house captain, unable to choose between us. And never did we imagine our friendship would unravel in such a way.

"I hate to admit it, but you brought out the best in me," he confessed.

"I think so, but I also don't think so," I hedged.

"You're blushing," he teased.

"No, I'm not," I protested.

"Yes, you are. Come on, admit it," he prodded.

"I don't engage in mental sparring with the unarmed. And no, I'm not," I quipped, a smile tugging at my lips.

Chuckling at my retort, he shifted the conversation to more serious matters.

"Mira, thanks for meeting me today. You've put my mind at ease. The thought of being rejected because of some flaw was eating me alive," he confessed.

"I'm glad you found peace. I hope I find mine too," I murmured.

"You will. Soon," he assured.

For all our previous conversations, this one felt different. I saw a side of Sarthak I hadn't before. He wasn't the mean-spirited adversary I'd known. I could empathize with him, and I couldn't shake the feeling that Missy should have married him. But what if I was wrong?

The next evening, we returned to Delhi, and by Monday, I was back to the daily grind. Lalita, ever the caring soul, brought me my coffee and inquired about my health. After a moment's hesitation, I offered a satisfactory response. That week, amidst curating others' content, I found solace in writing my own story for a prestigious magazine and getting to know Sarthak a little better.

Two weeks after my trip to Dalhousie, we began chatting. I learned he worked in an IT company in

Bangalore, and our late-night conversations became a comforting routine. Gradually, taunts turned to jokes, insults to banter.

He sent me snapshots of his office, his rented apartment, and various social gatherings. I always pestered him for a photo of himself, but he insisted the pleasure of seeing each other should be in person. It was the first thing we agreed on.

A year later, I landed a job at Deccan Herald in Bangalore, keeping it a secret from Sarthak for the ultimate surprise. My parents threw a lavish party to celebrate my success, inviting friends and family. Little did I know, fate had its own twisted surprise in store.

As Missy opened the door to unveil the surprise, the room erupted in cheers. But amidst the revelry, Missy dropped a bombshell.

"Mira, I'm getting married," she announced, her face beaming with joy.

"That's fantastic news! Is it the same man your Aunt Hema chose?" I inquired.

"No, I realized having a pure heart matters more than money," she confessed.

"Then who is it?" I pressed.

"Sarthak, of course," she revealed.

My head spun, my mind reeling in disbelief. How could Sarthak do this to me? He didn't even have the decency to tell me. Though we hadn't declared our love, this betrayal cut deep.

"Aren't you happy, Mira?" Missy's voice broke through my turmoil.

"Of course," I deadpanned, excusing myself for a glass of wine.

Minutes later, as I observed Missy giggling with a man in the corner, I knew exactly who he was. Applauding his audacity inwardly, I approached the happy couple.

"Hi, Sarthak," I greeted him, my tone cool.

"Hi, Mira. It's been ages since we talked, hasn't it?" he drawled, his words slurred with alcohol.

"What language are you speaking? Because it sounds like rubbish," I retorted.

"Whoa, calm down, Mirabai. Why are you so upset with me? Did I say something wrong?" he feigned innocence.

"We've been talking for over a year now, and you're claiming we haven't?" I countered, incredulous.

"Mirabai, you're proof that evolution can go in reverse! What's wrong with your memory? We met in Dalhousie. After that, I never contacted you or Missy. It was Missy's mother who fixed our meeting. Again." He clarified.

"So, you've been in Delhi this whole time?" I clarified.

"I never left Delhi," he confirmed.

"I think the wine's playing tricks on me. Excuse me," I faltered, escaping Sarthak's probing gaze.

A million thoughts raced through my mind. If Sarthak was here, who had I been talking to? Was this why he never shared a photo? But he seemed so genuine! And he knew everything about me. I messaged the (now) imposter, hoping for an explanation.

"Hey, what's going on?" I texted.

"Not much. Just at the office. Will call you later," came the response.

This only confirmed the imposter Sarthak's deception. Feeling vulnerable and attacked, I succumbed to the wine-induced haze and drifted off to sleep.

The next morning, I promptly blocked the imposter's number. Reporting him to the police seemed futile — after all, I had willingly engaged in conversation. He hadn't said anything offensive, nor had he made me uncomfortable. We simply chatted about everyday things. But the identity crisis loomed large.

I avoided the imposter for a week, focusing on settling into Bangalore. Fear and anxiety gripped me, leaving me paralyzed with indecision. Should I accept the job? Should I confront the imposter? The uncertainty distressed me.

A week after settling in Bangalore, my mind churned with uncertainty. Despite the job's satisfaction, questions gnawed at me like relentless mice. Should I confront the imposter? Should I accept the job and move on? The options danced like shadows in the corners of my consciousness, offering no clear path forward.

As the days passed, the allure of our late-night conversations lingered. My inbox overflowed with unanswered emails from the imposter, each one a reminder of the tangled web I found myself in.

Then, a sense of practicality washed over me like a cool breeze on a hot day. I realized dwelling on the imposter's identity served no purpose. The truth lay beyond my grasp, and chasing it would only lead to further confusion.

Instead, I focused on the tangible realities before me. My job at Deccan Herald offered opportunities for growth and fulfillment. I threw myself into my work, immersing myself in the rhythm of newspaper deadlines and journalistic pursuits.

As for the imposter, I chose to let go of the tangled threads of our digital connection. Blocking his number and moving forward felt like closing a chapter in a book I never intended to read again.

With each passing day, I found solace in the familiar routines of my new life in Bangalore. The city welcomed me with open arms, its vibrant energy a balm for my restless soul.

And though questions lingered in the corners of my mind, I found comfort in the knowledge that some mysteries are best left unsolved. For now, I embraced the present moment, letting go of the past and trusting in the journey ahead.

Salad Days

Light filtered through the translucent white curtains as if inviting presence which had long been missing in the room. Whilst shadows danced on the ceiling, the floor screamed in loneliness. It had been a month since my grandmother had passed away. Strangely, her room still smelt the same- a stale, musty odour with a tinge of something as acrid as mothballs. It was typical of an old person's smell.

The room, a haven of comfort and nostalgia, told the tale of a life well-lived. Adorned in a tapestry of hues, the walls were dressed in wallpaper that seemed to have captured the essence of a vintage garden, where blossoms of roses and daisies intertwined in a dance frozen in time. Sunlight streamed through the lace curtains, casting a soft, warm glow upon weathered wooden furniture that proudly displayed the marks of time's passage.

In the heart of the room, a study table stood—a relic of a lifetime's pursuit of knowledge and quiet reflection. Crafted from sturdy wood, the table bore the elegant marks of time, etched into its polished surface like the lines on a wise face. Over the years, it became a repository of cherished memories and a testament to resilience. Several photo frames stood like soldiers in attention- still and quiet.

There was so much joy. Love, too. In all those photographs. The romantic walks under the moonlit sky, the candle-light dinners, the extravagance of splendid secret meetings where my granny was showered with love and affection- all speaking volumes about her dreams and desires coming to fruition. How I wished I was that fortunate!

By the window, a well-loved armchair, its once-vibrant upholstery softened by the caress of time, invited repose. It sat beside a small table, upon which a teacup rested, grinning in pride with the tea stains left behind like scars on the foot of the cup. Beyond the window lay a serene garden, a symphony of greenery and vibrant blooms that swayed in the gentle breeze, offering a picturesque tableau.

A magnificent mahogany bookshelf, standing proudly against a wall, bore the weight of a lifetime's worth of stories. Its shelves, bowed ever so slightly under the weight of cherished tomes, beckoned exploration into realms both real and imagined. Each book held its own story, its own adventure, waiting patiently to be rediscovered. But my grandmother never advocated reading. She disliked it. Instead, she would perch on her bed like a bird on a branch and indulge in a never-ending time-lapse of watching television.

The air carried a delicate fragrance — a soothing blend of lavender and memories — a testament to the potpourri nestled on the bedside table. An old-fashioned clock, its brass hands ticking away the moments in a steady rhythm, stood sentinel beside the bed, marking the passage of time with unwavering constancy.

In this room, time had seemed to stand still, cradling within its embrace a treasure trove of experiences and wisdom. It was a space where every corner, every trinket, and every ray of light whispered the tale of a life well-lived, painting a portrait of cherished moments and enduring grace.

In the serene embrace of my grandmother's room, memories unfolded like the delicate petals of a bygone era. A vintage dressing table stood in a quiet corner, adorned with a curated collection of perfume bottles and an array of black-and-white photographs, each a testament to a chapter in her extraordinary life.

As I ventured into the nostalgic trove, my attention gravitated towards a group photo adorning the dresser. The subdued tones of sepia unveiled a tableau from my grandmother's youth, capturing the essence of an era lost in the folds of time. Amidst the smiling faces, her gaze held a captivating allure, fixating on a young boy positioned at the extreme right of the photograph.

Intrigued by this enigmatic figure, I couldn't help but wonder if he was the protagonist of my grandmother's timeless love story – my grandfather. Seeking confirmation, I turned to my mother, only to unravel a tale adorned with the hues of a gentle romance. The young boy in the photograph wasn't my grandfather but, rather, my grandmother's crush, a clandestine narrative woven delicately into the rich tapestry of her youth.

As I stood amidst the relics of her life, the room transformed into a sacred space where each artefact whispered stories of a time long ago. The photograph, with its sepia-kissed charm, became a window into a chapter of my grandmother's history, resonating with the timeless echo of affection and the tender stirrings of youthful admiration. The air in the room seemed to carry the soft murmur of bygone days, and at that moment, I felt connected to the romance that had unfolded against the backdrop of my grandmother's dresser.

The relentless yearning to unravel the tale of my grandmother's lost love haunted my every waking moment and seeped into the stillness of my nights. It became an insatiable quest, a journey through the echoes of her memories that seemed to elude me like whispers carried by the wind. And then, as if orchestrated by fate itself, a fortuitous night unfolded, ushering me into the heart of the mystery that lingered in her room.

In the soft glow of the moonlight, I found myself drawn once again to the sanctuary of her space, seeking solace amid the sweet nothings that held the essence of her presence. As my fingers grazed the surface of her belongings, navigating the labyrinth of artefacts, my heart held a delicate hope that this night might reveal the elusive fragments of her untold love story.

And there it was—a big trunk tucked away in the corner, overshadowed by the myriad of other mementoes that concealed its significance. Intrigued, I carefully opened the trunk, revealing a treasure trove of forgotten relics. Nestled within, like a precious gem waiting to be discovered, was a diary wrapped in a yellow cloth and secured with a red silk ribbon. It was a clandestine haven of secrets, patiently waiting to unfold the chapters of my grandmother's heart.

The mere sight of the diary ignited a mix of emotions—excitement, trepidation, and a profound sense of connection to a narrative that had remained shrouded in the folds of time. As I delicately untied the silk ribbon, each gentle movement resonated with the anticipation of uncovering the intimate musings that had been preserved with great care.

In the hushed ambience of her room, I began to leaf through the pages, each stroke of ink revealing a fragment of her soul. The words danced on the pages, recounting a love story that transcended the years. My grandmother's emotions spilt onto the paper, creating an intimate tapestry that wove the narrative of her lost love. In that sacred moment, I felt a profound connection with her, as if the whispers of her untold story had finally found a listener in the stillness of the night.

In a distorted form of Hindi, my grandmother had jotted down her feelings.

I

In the tapestry of my youth, Ekram's entry was a stroke of fate, painting our lives with hues that resonated with the vibrancy of love. Our story unfolded in hushed tones and stolen glances, within the sacred walls of our school.

One day, during a Literature class, Ekram's words wove poetry that echoed the depth of his soul. His eloquence left me spellbound, and our shared passion for Literature became the foundation of an unspoken connection.

"The beauty of words is in their ability to transcend boundaries. Don't you think?" He asked me.

"Indeed. They create bridges where hearts can meet."

"Do you ever feel like words can bridge the gaps between worlds?" He breathed as he cupped my hands into his, a gentle smile gracing his lips.

"Maybe, if the world were as simple as a well-crafted sentence." I moaned.

Our encounters, though discreet, blossomed into a love that defied societal norms. Stolen glances turned into furtive meetings, and our shared smiles spoke a language only the heart comprehended.

"Do you believe in destiny?" He queried once.

"Maybe destiny led us to this moment."

"Our hearts seem to be entangled in this unspoken connection."

"Sometimes, the unspoken says more than words ever could." Like a perfect jigsaw puzzle, my words found the right resting spot. It was as if my heart guided me to complete his incompleteness.

Yet, as our love flourished, so did the shadows of societal expectations. Whispers of disapproval echoed around us, casting doubt on the viability of our connection.

"Our hearts know no boundaries, but the world does," he announced on one fateful day.

The inevitable realization dawned upon us – our love faced a crucible of challenges, primarily the stark disparity in our religious backgrounds. The choice to part ways, though agonizing, seemed inevitable.

"Ekram, our love is like a delicate flower, but society sees it as a thorn. We must tread carefully."

"I never imagined love would come with such a heavy price."

And so, we made the heart-wrenching decision to part ways, our love story finding its conclusion amidst the harsh realities of our time.

"Perhaps, in another time and place..."

"Our love will linger, a poignant melody in the symphony of our memories."

As I inscribe these words, the echoes of our dialogues reverberate in the chambers of my heart – a testament to a love that dared to exist in the face of societal constraints.

II

In the labyrinth of time, the echoes of Ekram's love lingered, a bittersweet symphony that reverberated through the corridors of my heart. Barely managing to pick up the fragments of my shattered emotions, I embarked on a journey where the wishes of my parents held sway, and practicality became the compass guiding my steps.

Sometimes, moving on becomes the only choice, even if the heart protests.

The days blurred into a monotonous routine until a new chapter unfolded, introducing me to a man named Rajender, who would soon become the anchor of my life. In the midst of practicalities, he appeared as a comforting shore, and our dialogues held the promise of a future intertwined with shared dreams.

"Your laughter is like a melody, bringing warmth to even the coldest days," Rajender would shower praises so very often.

Maybe it's the echoes of a forgotten tune- my heart would respond.

As the days turned into months, and months into years, Raj's presence became a steady rhythm, soothing the remnants of my heart that still echoed with Ekram's memory.

"We are like two stars, destined to share the same sky."

"Yet, my heart carries the shadow of another star that once shone brightly," I never dared to say.

The decision to marry Raj was not a surrender to societal expectations but a realization that in his love, I found a haven of stability. His dialogues became the verses of a new chapter, carrying with them the fragrance of acceptance and companionship.

"Your eyes hold the magic of a thousand stories."

"But behind these stories, there lies a tale that time couldn't erase," my silent whispers never reached his ears.

Our marriage became a canvas where new memories were painted, yet the shadows of Ekram's love were woven into its fabric. In those nostalgic dialogues, I found solace, acknowledging that while Ekram set an unmatched standard, Raj's love was a melody that gently healed the wounds of a past love.

If grandmother was alive, she'd have probably shared this story with me at some point. It was just a matter of looking beyond the obvious and noticing the smaller details. 'Nostalgic Embrace' is what she had called this episode in her diary. 'Salad Days' is what she'd have called it now - the days of being young and inexperienced.

As I gathered the scattered layers of intangible emotions, my heart yearned to know what had become of Ekram, the man who had once had a chance of loving and being loved by a timeless and resilient lover. Probably grandmother would have liked to know about him too. With a newfound desire to find the name in the plethora of possibilities, I exited the room, shutting behind me not just any mahogany door but temporarily closing a gate that could sustain an incessant torrent.

Enakshi J.

Good Riddance

Damn. I was late. Again.

The addictive thriller on Netflix was to be blamed. Like a delivery boy crisscrossing on a bike to deliver pizza in thirty minutes, I navigated the heavy traffic of Bangalore with ease. Only the bumper of my bike had to face the music! But I was safe. Not sound though. Damn was my new favourite word. Everything in my life was going unplanned.

While the anticipation of how the day would be gripped my mind, my body fell victim to a collateral collision with the glass door. *How reckless of me!*

"Again?" caterwauled Sana.

The words pierced through the cacophony of noises and hit my ego. *Again.*

"You? Again?" I managed to retort.

"Yes, of course. Good always co-exists with evil. So, how can I allow you to stand in solitude?" She whispered. Thankfully, it was subtle enough for the rest of the people walking past us.

"Oh, because nothing says companionship like a constant sidekick of evil, right?" I managed.

"Would you both shut up already?"

The voice made us both turn our heads together. It was Bobby, my friend cum colleague from the same department as mine.

"Right in the morning, really? If not yours, at least care for our peace! Stop spewing venom at each other!" He reprimanded.

Eyeing his glittery jacket with suspicion, Sana was first to speak.

"I'd shout 'Good Riddance' the day Jessica fires both of you. Such a relief it would be!"

"As if…" I was cut short by Bobby again.

"Ignore, Arnie. Let's go."

Sana had been my arch-nemesis since school. Our perspectives never aligned, whether it was the school's annual day dance or the basketball match. Every little thing became a battleground where we clashed, not to establish the correctness of our views but to emerge victorious in the argument. You know, the usual ego tussle. While I thought I'd get rid of her after the 12th, my unlucky stars were adamant about making my life more challenging. Consequently, we landed jobs at the same firm. It wouldn't come as a surprise that we went to the same college too. Thank God the departments were different. But hostile life has its share of woes. For me, it was seeing her every single day at the cafeteria, engaging in verbal diarrhoea and then regretting the mental exhaustion that would follow.

And then at Brent's Branding Agency, we were at each other's throats, ready to slice apart with verbal menace. People despised our banters but liked our work ethics. We're good. Really good at our jobs. Sana was heading the Designing and I led the Advertising. Contrary to how most people viewed me as the one who prioritized ego over sympathy, I did have a little heart when it came to watching my words before letting them free. Sana, not ever. Her words came without any filter. She'd scatter ban and spread ruin, both in merely minutes. Pure talent, I must say. But what's also true was that she was a talented graphic designer with a flair for minimal aesthetics, and I was a persuasive advertising expert. Poles apart!

It was a week before Christmas that I found myself reluctantly paired with her for an upcoming project. The challenge at hand was to craft a visual identity and promotional campaign for a cutting-edge tech conference. With conflicting styles and opposing views on what constitutes effective design, our collaboration promised failure.

"How will we work on this together? I mean with Sana? You don't have anyone else?" I shot an array of questions at Jessica, the manager.

"The project demands a seamless fusion of Sana's penchant for minimalist aesthetics and your flair for attention-grabbing concepts. The outcome needs to be a captivating blend of innovation and visual appeal, reflecting both the sophistication of the tech industry and the excitement of the conference's agenda. So, you two are my best bets!"

Silence was my answer, for I knew I was talking to the wall. What followed was the verbal jousting between the two of us, Sana and I, setting the stage for a creative clash that might just birth something disastrous!

"Oh, great, another brilliant concept from the advertising genius. Did you use all your creativity on that one, or is this the pinnacle of your brilliance?" remarked Sana immediately after I finished my rough pitch.

"Coming from someone who thinks Comic Sans is a masterpiece, I'll take that as a compliment. At least my designs don't look like they belong in the '90s."

"Well, excuse me for not jumping on the neon and glitter bandwagon. Your ideas are like a bad pop song – catchy for a moment, but ultimately forgettable."

"And yours are like a grayscale nightmare – dull, lifeless, and everyone wishes they could just fast-forward through it."

There was a sudden screech. It was Bobby. We had been so busy arguing that we didn't realize when Jessica vanished into thin air!

"Horrific. You two are incorrigible. Jessica was upset with your behaviour. Leaving the two of you in a room is equivalent to leaving a jaguar and an anaconda together!"

"Well, assuming I'm the jaguar, I hope you don't plan on devouring my creativity," accused Sana.

"Devouring creativity? Please, your designs are more like a house cat trying to be fierce," I surmised.

"House cat? At least my work doesn't slither its way into mediocrity like your flashy ads."

"Flashy? You call it flashy; I call it attention-grabbing – something your designs could use a lesson in."

"Attention-grabbing, just like a snake charmer trying to distract everyone from the lack of substance in your campaigns."

"Lack of substance? Your graphics are so minimal; they make a haiku look verbose."

"Well, I'd take a haiku over the visual cacophony of your designs any day. At least poetry has structure."

"Structure? Your designs need structure more than my pet snake needs a ballet lesson."

As the banter continued, the office atmosphere crackled with humour and tension, creating a peculiar dynamic that had the entire team on the edge of their seats. Bobby couldn't take it anymore.

"STOP IT. GET OUT. IMMEDIATELY,"

Some more days and long nights followed. But our mouths never got tired. What was strange was we never argued after the discussions. Genial greetings were common. Sometimes, evening tea was on cards. And there, we never spoke about work. The conversations were personal. About families. About relationships. About life outside the office. Dare I say school! And upon reflection, I realized how only work was our battlefield.

After that day's extraordinary performance, convincing Jessica to lend a patient ear was next to impossible. Appalled. That's what she was. I wasn't sorry. Nor was Sana. After all, only the best gets to win. Not two.

Against his frustration, Bobby became our saviour and managed to get Jessica inside the conference room one evening. History was repeated or better, created. In a pastel green midi, Sana volunteered to go first. Her designs were plain. Mundane too. But Jessica seemed to like them. My ego got the better of me. This time, I started the war.

"Graphic design must be easy for you; after all, Photoshop can do all the heavy lifting and you can chill while it covers up the lack of substance in your work."

"Unlike you, I don't sell dreams that no one wants. Your ads are like clickbait – promising something exciting, but delivering disappointment. I bet even your morning coffee is as bitter as your attitude."

"Well, I'd rather have a bitter coffee than a tasteless design. Maybe if you spent less time adjusting the saturation on your filters, you'd understand what real creativity is."

She didn't answer. It pinched me. I expected her to fight back. But why? Didn't I win the argument inarguably?

As for Jessica, she had to do what she had to do. We were given a final deadline to present the pitch after the next three days. Only this time not verbally but through a visual aid.

The task wasn't difficult and I should've been happy about it. Yet I wasn't. An incomprehensible emotional turmoil took control of my mind. Like an unwelcome force wringing my gut. It was unbearable. Frustrating too. I wanted to know what was the reason.

There was no time though.

Working late into the night, every other day, I noticed a peculiar transformation taking root within me. Since fatigue wore down our defences, candid conversations replaced guarded exchanges. Shared laughter over shared frustrations slowly eroded the animosity that had defined our relationship.

In a surprising turn of events, I discovered common interests and shared experiences from our school days, a topic we never really discussed. Unveiling layers of her personality that had long been concealed, I realized that the roots of my initial disdain ran shallow compared to the newfound connection I was fostering.

Initially, Sana's unconventional and seemingly structured design approach clashed with my chaotic advertising mindset, creating a dissonance in our collaborative efforts. However, as we delved into the intricacies of our shared project, I couldn't ignore the fervour and passion emanating from her graphic designs. It was akin to witnessing an immaculate organization, where each stroke held a captivating narrative. Gradually, I found myself admiring the vivacious energy she injected into our usually unorderly workspace. Sana's unwavering commitment to her creative vision unfolded as a testament to her dedication. Amidst our playful banter and artistic sparring, I discovered a profound attraction to the determination reflected in her eyes, to the steadfast belief she held in the power of her designs. Against all odds, our contrasting approaches sparked a realization – beneath the surface-level clashes lay a shared dedication to our respective realms of creativity. It was then, amidst the collision of divergent aesthetics, that the Anaconda acknowledged the magnetic allure of the Jaguar.

Fortunately, I began to sense a subtle shift in her demeanour too. Her once bold and assertive exchanges took on a nuanced tone, revealing glimpses of a shared sentiment that mirrored my evolving feelings. Amid our creative sparring, I caught her stealing glances, and a hint of a smile surfaced during moments of agreement. Sana's usually confident demeanour faltered occasionally, betraying a vulnerability that echoed the uncertainty of mutual emotions. A carefully placed compliment, a lingering gaze – these subtle gestures hinted at a reciprocity that lingered in the air. Yet, uncertainty gnawed at me. Was it genuine affection or merely a byproduct of our intense collaboration? The lines between professional banter and personal sentiment blurred, leaving me grappling with the question of whether the allure I felt was reciprocated or merely a product of our creatively charged environment. As the magnetic pull of our contrasting worlds continued, I found myself navigating uncharted territory, unsure of whether Sana's heart echoed the same enigmatic melody that played in mine.

The D-day arrived. Too soon. Ready and confident, we submitted the video for approval. Without a doubt, it was a hit. After all, it was a result of two brilliant minds at work! Honestly, I never thought I'd share success with anyone. Especially Sana.

As a reward for my better understanding, I invited her to the coffee house just across the corner. I was prepared for the showdown. Whether it would end in a verbattle or into something more meaningful, I didn't care. I just had to get rid of the tension that haunted my body and mind every single time I came close to her. Her scent sent shivers down my spine. In the cold light of day, I realised that the hatred had transformed into love. Good riddance to the barriers of professional detachments!

"Arnav, brace yourself – the grand finale is upon us. Our final presentation, a masterpiece born from the chaotic collaboration of a jaguar and an anaconda." She revelled.

"Brace myself? Please, Sana, your idea of chaos is rearranging icons on your desktop. My advertising prowess adds the real flair." I hypothesized, happy that my Jaguar was back in form.

"Flair? Your campaigns are so flashy; people blink and miss the message. But let's not quibble. I've added a touch of sophistication to your flashy world – a visual symphony of sleek minimalism."

"Sleek minimalism? Your designs are like a slow burn – dragging on, leaving people wondering when it will end."

"Okay, stop. Why are we fighting?" She softened.

"I don't know."

"Let's just stop. I know you hate me but just pretend you don't. Okay?" She sighed.

"Who said that? I thought you hated me." I confided.

"I never said that." She spluttered.

"But you never say a lot of things. Unlike you, I think I will be the bold one here today."

"What does that mean?"

"Sana, amidst our clash of creative titans, there's something I've realized. Your brilliance isn't just in your designs; it's in the strategy that fuels them. And, well, it has sparked something in me too – something unexpected."

"Oh, do tell, Mr. Flashy."

"Call it what you will, but I think our collaboration could extend beyond the office chaos. What if we bring a little sophistication into our lives outside these walls?"

"Sophistication? Are you proposing a partnership or an art exhibit?"

"Let's call it a revolution of the heart. How about we celebrate our grand finale in this coffee haven with a touch of personal flair? A little flash, a dash of minimalism, and maybe a hint of intrigue?"

She was surprised. Shocked even. I was scared. But I had heard of the leap of faith before. And jumping never sounded more fun!

"And, Sana, perhaps we could explore the uncharted territory of, well, something beyond professional collaborations. A territory where each stroke on the canvas holds a promise of more."

"Arnav, you're really pushing the boundaries here, but maybe a little revolution isn't a bad thing."

It took a while to comprehend her subtle hint. I knew I was skating on thin ice. Still, the snowball effect was unexpected!

"Sometimes, Sana, the boldest moves create the most beautiful masterpieces. Maybe our canvas isn't just confined to pixels and campaigns."

"You're suggesting a canvas that extends beyond the office walls?"

"Precisely. A canvas where each stroke tells a story, and the colours we choose are the moments we create together."

"Arnav, this is like a whole new realm for us. Are you sure we won't end up turning our masterpiece into a messy collage?"

"Life is messy, Sana. But it's the unexpected splashes of colour that make it beautiful. Let's venture into this new chapter and see where our strokes lead us."

"As much as I'm willing to surrender to fate, I'm scared of my mind. I know you too well."

"That's a good thing, silly! We wouldn't have to spend time knowing each other. We can begin by loving each other unconditionally."

"You're making this sound like a fairy tale, Arnav."

"Well, they say life imitates art, and I think our collaboration is about to paint a pretty enchanting picture."

"What exactly are you proposing, Mr. Bold Moves?"

"A dance, Sana. A dance through this uncharted territory we're stepping into."

Within seconds, I twirled her into my arms. The turmoil vanished. The knot melted away. Good riddance! Soon enough, the coffee shop around us faded into the background, leaving only a rhythm of our shared heartbeats. As our gaze lingered, I leaned in, afraid still, capturing Sana's lips in a gentle kiss- the culmination of our banter, the strokes of our connection, and the beginning of a romantic journey beyond the creative chaos of our professional lives.

The Quixotic Vacation

Life is too short for fake butter or fake people.

But life's really worth it for this individual who has been holding my hand in his palms for over half an hour. As the warmth of his veined, slender hands seep into my very being, my eyes shut for that brief moment in a hasty attempt to hide my feelings. I have known Ankit for what, just a year, yet time seems to have progressed swiftly since we first met.

I met Ankit at the rescue centre where we both had fallen for Bruno, the brown pup. We decided to share custody by alternating our time with him. And that's how we got a chance to share more about each other too. A workaholic by nature, Ankit often skipped lunch owing to deadline pressure but I was the opposite. I ensured that I ate on time to remain energized. With such trivial dissimilarities, we realized that we were the missing pieces of a jigsaw puzzle, the pieces that fit right into each other. Our chat sessions would go on for hours and we would never be exhausted or deprived of content to talk about. As luck might have it, I fell for him soon enough but feared sharing my true feelings. Rejection is distressing. But who knew that Ankit had been harbouring similar feelings for me too? When invited to a common friend's cocktail party, we both readily agreed. Bored of the drama that was alien to us, we decided to book an Uber and head out. Unfortunately, another friend chipped in and urged us to take him along. And now, here we are describing our first meeting with Amit, the third wheel in our story at the moment.

"Since the first time I saw him, I knew we would click together," I beamed.

"Such strange encounters don't last long, Shreya. You both should take things slow. Have you both proposed to each other already?" I could imagine myself strangling Amit's neck because of his absurd advice. But still, Ankit hadn't proposed to me. And that thought lingered.

Reading my silence, Ankit tapped my bare shoulder from the backseat making me turn towards him. He gestured towards my hand, cupped my left hand, kissed it tight, selected my slender ring finger and inserted a diamond ring.

"What did you just do?" I asked.

"You know what I did," he cajoled.

"You need to propose first," I demanded.

"I will do that now. "

"You've got the order of events wrong," I frowned.

"Propose doesn't necessarily mean asking for marriage only. It can also imply that someone is ready to put forth a plan or suggestion," he articulated.

Before even I could open my mouth to scold him, he hushed me.

"You must allow me to tell you how ardently I admire and love you. You are too generous to trifle with me. If your feelings are still what they were last April, tell me so at once. My affections and wishes are unchanged, but one word from you will silence me on this subject forever."

"Why do these words sound familiar?" I wondered.

"Last April?" I questioned.

"Bruno's custody had started an argument between us in April, remember? And I have been thinking if you have moved on from that point or not. Do you hate me still for wanting to take Bruno?"

"Are you mad? If I were mad at you, I wouldn't be sharing custody, spending time and socializing with friends with you. Of course, I adore you too. I'm in love with you, and I'm not in the business of denying myself the simple pleasure of saying true things."

What?" I asked.

"Nothing," he said.

"Why are you looking at me like that?"

Ankit half smiled. "Because you're beautiful. I enjoy looking at beautiful people and I decided a while ago not to deny myself the simpler pleasures of existence."

I couldn't control my mind wandering in two different directions. One, I was bursting with joy and immense pleasure. My heart was lit up like a thousand bulbs atop a dark mountain. Two, Ankit's flirting sounded familiar. I could anticipate his next words. And that scared me.

Sensing my uneasiness, he cupped my hand again and asked me to promise him that I would never leave him and go. Or he would die.

The time froze before I could respond. There was a shower of white light which caused excruciating pain in my eyes. My body ached and my lips became parched. The next thing I remembered was green pastures of freshly cut grass, the yellow sign board showing off 'Clemens' Wellness Centre' written in bold and a toppled wheelchair lying by my side. Before I could shout for help, I saw a nurse rushing towards me. She mouthed, "Oh, no, again?" and it all came running back to me.

Augustus, Darcy and Landon were pushed back into the pages of the books that had fallen off my lap. Their words lingered. Ankit's face had become blurred by then. His speech, or rather Darcy's and Augustus' words, made no sense then.

"Whom did you meet this time?" Chuckled the nurse, my only friend in the centre.

"Ankit from Mumbai," I answered and laughed at my own miserable mind that never gave me any respite from playing these games. It's not its fault either. It's the fault of my stars. The stars beckoned my uncle to emotionally abuse me after my parents' accident. The stars that made me handicapped. The stars took away my motive to wish for anything good or worthy of living a happy life. But Serra, my nurse, shared an ounce of wisdom with me once. She suggested that I record every imaginary meeting of mine in a black journal- a keepsake for bad days. And so, I followed the habit, signalling her to hand over the journal and became ready to collect my thoughts.

The longest distance between two places is time. Even miles might feel shorter if your journey towards your destination is hindered by time. The more time you spend experiencing a potluck of emotions, the more difficult it becomes to stay calm and wait for the climax. As I write this inside my charred black notebook, I realize how futile this trip has been. No, not the literal travelling; mine is the travel in time. My marvellous mind works this way- bizarre encounters, implausible rendezvous and unsustainable relationships.

Every time I am brought back to the mundane world where relationships perish, people change and moments fizzle out, I am left in an uncharted territory from which escape seems impossible. My mind, though, is in a more miserable state. Yet again knowing that the adventurous encounter with another stranger, who felt so real, is a repercussion of my vivid imagination is painful. Hurtful even. And now all I can do is sit idly on this machine while it takes me around the straggling fence at the click of this small button. And wait for my next moment of zoning out. And simultaneously curse my dissociative identity crisis. And stop, stare and just be helplessly entertained by the prospect of meeting or knowing another fictional being. After all, life's too short for fake butter or such fake people.

The Whimsical Flautist

The mellifluous notes were blinding sweet. Deliciously enjoyable. So much so that I didn't realize that I had been sipping air from my Frooti Tetra pack for the last fifteen minutes. My eyes had found a resting spot. His face. Contortions spread across like the layers of tar on a new road, his nostrils flaring every time an ounce of energy was spent blowing into the flute. The music swelled my heart; it pierced through several layers of flesh and touched my soul. Caught in a trance, I had lost control of my senses. And surprisingly, this joy that I felt was pure ecstasy. It wasn't love. It wasn't infatuation. It was just soul-stirring music playing cupid in this improbable story of getting to know each other.

Addiction is bad. And this music, just after one class of therapy, became my drug. However, as much as I convinced myself not to attend the live show again, my heart became an obstinate child who could throw tantrums about not being given importance. Consequently, there I was, seated in the second row, only this time a little closer to the flautist. There wasn't any air traffic between his gaze and mine. I was mindful not to get carried away and give the benefit of the doubt because establishing eye contact with the audience would only help him perform better. But my reasons were different. Vaguely genuine. Kind of ethical too. With a flutter in my stomach every time his gaze met mine, I pressed the gentlest smile upon my lips, making sure I did not let my guard down. He was kind enough to return the gesture with a subtle nod. This subtle reciprocation fuelled my desire to know this person more. Talk to him. Appreciate him. Maybe over a cup of coffee?

Swiftly moving his fingers over the notches of the instrument, he tapped the right chord of my heart when the instrumental interlude was doing its job of enthralling the crowd. Keshav, the name that would now remain in my mind whenever I would listen to Indian classical music, had my soul in his grip. What beauty he created with his music! It compelled my very being to beg for more. More of his music. More tranquillity. More of eternal bliss. For the first time, I realized how good music can make you its slave. I sat transfixed by the melodious notes and then he did what I hadn't expected him to do. Raising his left eyebrow, he gestured a 'hi' my way. All while playing the golden flute. Frozen and startled, I couldn't respond. While my mind scattered ban at my helpless yet desperate heart, my hand took the reigns of my destiny and waved back at the person who had possibly been successful at sweeping me off my feet. But I was being way too filmy! I had to let this brew. More aroma, more encounters and more exchange of words might just add the right flavour. Probably another visit would help. And yes, that's what I did. The third day of the week I was like a diligent student sitting on the first bench, waiting anxiously for her new teacher to begin the class!

Expectations can often push you towards the very edge of the cliff, for their weight is so immense that it can drown you in the abyss. My experience with Keshav and his music had been good so far but I was expecting more. More of music, more of acquaintances and more of him. Even though my mother had shown signs of disapproval when I had suggested that she come along with me to this show for the third time, I knew that my decision had to be right. The gut feeling, as they say, was strong. As the doors of the big hall shut close, I breathed in the cacophony of noises. And then, just within a flash second, he appeared on the stage. Wearing an uptight waistcoat, paired neatly with black trousers, he looked immaculate. His muscular hands held the flute tight. How I wished I was the flute and that he was close. How I wished I knew him more! How I wished I had met him earlier! But wishes are not always granted, are they? He took his spot, the same old corner with a spotlight, and then he began. Shivers ran through my body as each note of music brushed past my body. Hypnotizing. Engaging. Magnificent. His medley of music made my heart crumble to bits like how one feels upon summiting a great height or finding an old memory box. I revelled in my own small achievement. The achievement of being able to see him again.

The reverberations encapsulated the hall. My constant gaze at him would have definitely landed me into trouble but he was no less. He reciprocated with a smile this time. Acknowledgement is important I know but smile? His lips curved into a crescent upon finding me in the front row and I'm not sure if I actually saw him mouthing something. It can't be. He cannot possibly whisper something during the performance. I must be hallucinating! And then, the last bit of the interlude began. Poignance and grace became permanent residents of that hall as Keshav took over his flauto traverso, caressing every nook and corner of the wooden hollow with his bare fingers. Soon, everything else faded, drowned in a mystical realm that shouted peace.

That day, before I could mark my exit from the hall, I decided to give it a try by making a first move. Consequently, I waited with bated breath for the musicians to gather backstage, in the hope of getting fortunate enough to talk to him. As luck would have it, he was nowhere to be found.

"Can I have 2 minutes with the flautist, Keshav?" I enquired the giant man whose black overalls scared the daylights out of me.

"I'm sorry, ma'am, he's not here. He left for the airport immediately after the show got over."

Alas! That seemed like a rushed conclusion to my story, didn't it? But I couldn't do anything about it. I was not Salman Khan or Hrithik Roshan to go to the airport and confess my feelings. I had no feelings per se. I wasn't sure whether it was his charisma or his music that acted as my magnetic field. Whatever it was, it was gone. And I was back to reality as if I had just come back from a luxurious vacation.

Three months later

The balmy air of March wasn't helping much. Even though Bangalore was beautifully decked by florals all around, the musty atmosphere reduced the ease of working in an enclosed space. My second art gallery was up and live. Bangaloreans were entering the large auditorium with zestful and eager eyes. I had prayed hard for this event to be successful; I could really use the money to replenish my art supplies. At 30, merely painting my heart on a white canvas wasn't really helping me pay the bills.

I would be lying if I said that I never thought of reaching out to Keshav. In fact, I had stalked him for the longest time on all the social media handles yet some distinct apprehension had acted as an inhibitor. Probably I was scared of realizing that all the reciprocation was a concocted tale of fancy events. Often one gets jitters when it's time to learn the truth. I also felt the same. Yet there I was listening to his music on my earphones while munching the energy bar. After all, his music was my drug!

"Someone is looking for you, madam," the attendant tapped my door.

"Who? A buyer?" I vacillated.

"Doesn't look like one. He seems to be more famous than just being a regular art enthusiast," deadpanned the attendant.

I was intrigued. Having someone well-known attend my gallery could bring brighter prospects. Hence, I headed out, carelessly wiping my mouth off the leftovers.

"Hi," is what I wanted to say. But the cat got my tongue. There he stood, as immaculate as ever, looking spatially all around himself, probably appreciating my work and nodding in wonder.

"Hello, Ms. Mysterious," he gently intoned.

"Ms. What?" I sounded ridiculous.

"Well, didn't you leave that day without meeting me? And all these three months I have been on my feet trying to figure out who you were. If it were not for your Facebook Event, I wouldn't have had a chance to meet you. I'm Keshav. I'm sure you remember me." He spluttered and bit his lower lip.

"Of course, I know you. How can I not? I attended…"

"…my live show thrice in a row. I know." He cut me short and smiled.

"I had tried to meet you backstage but you had left. Disappointed and helpless, I had let that moment pass."

"You should have shown some resilience. I'm quite active on social media. You could have found me there. Messaged me. Pinged me. Reached out."

I didn't know how to respond. My mind was caught in the spiral of the addictive musical interlude. My body had stopped cooperating. I didn't know what I was expected to do. Or say. My eyes found this temporary moment of paralysis enjoyable and rested upon his lips as he enunciated a few more words. All feeble whispers for me now. Here was the flautist who had stolen my soul with his music. And here was I, the mad artist who had already started painting a fairytale in my mind.

"You're freaking out. Don't freak out," he fretted.

"No, I'm not."

"I know I'm not supposed or expected to be here. Yet I wanted to know for myself. It is my faith that you were impressed by my music and that you might be slightly interested in knowing more about me."

"Your faith seems to hit the bull's eye. You're exceptional with your flute. There's a different kind of trance that I was transported to when I heard you for the first time. It was like being unintentionally drawn to you."

"So, you do speak your mind. Then I'm glad I came."

"I'm glad too," it was my time to reciprocate. In casual blue jeans and a brick-coloured t-shirt, his charm was too much to handle already. I forgot the values of altruism and decided to bag the opportunity that had walked my way.

"Would you like to talk over a cup of coffee after I wind up here?"

"Actually, I was thinking of dinner. That would give us more time, " he winked.

"Bring along your flute, for I might test your skills," I joked.

"I might not just be skilled at playing the flute, you know."

"Oh yes, absolutely. You're skilled at stalking. How else would you know where to find me," I tried hard to sound funny.

"That Facebook Event page had your picture pasted on the cover image. That's how I found you. You know, you could have played wisely." A smile escaped the corner of his mouth as if taunting me for flaunting my wit.

Failing miserably at concealing my surprise, I decided to hold my horses before blurting out something irrelevant. He took the lead and told me how he had noticed my presence on the very first day. "There was something whimsical about the way you looked at me while I played the flute," he mentioned.

I expressed how deeply affected I was by his composition and that it had had a lasting effect on me. I became more aware of his world in the evening when we had dinner together. Things were just so easy with him. Seamless. Genuine. Vaguely liberating. He was a patient listener to my incessant chatter and our worlds of art found solace in each other's company. Though he's originally from Mumbai, he promised to meet often because Bangaloreans rooted for his music. Therefore, I proposed a joint venture- his concert and my exhibition together. He agreed. I applauded my luck for kickstarting my (fairy)tale on such a note. I felt happy.

Untethered Hearts

The restaurant hummed with the sounds of clinking cutlery and hushed conversations. It was a popular spot for both casual outings and special occasions. On this particular evening, two lives were about to intersect in unexpected ways.

I sat at a table near the window, my eyes scanning the room ever and anon as I waited for my client to arrive. Immaculately dressed, my occasional tapping on the table was enough to make my fresh manicure evident. Impatience. Annoyance. Guilt. I felt all three at the same time. I despised the idea of letting time win. Every minute was crucial for me. No, I wasn't a rat in the race. It was more a result of my eccentricity that led me to become so profoundly involved in work and invest every precious second into doing something that would fetch remarkable results.

As a renowned lawyer, I was often sought after for my legal consultation. Tonight, I was meeting a client who needed advice on a complex case. When the client couldn't be spotted by my peripheral vision, I decided to refresh my memory and go through the file. Again. Lost in thought, flipping through my notes, my inward eye suddenly became aware of someone's gaze. A tall, handsome man had just walked in and he was nearing my table. As our eyes locked for a brief moment, a wild spark ignited my spirit and prompted it to soar. Every nerve cell in my body screamed in confusion. There was an uncanny acquaintance that propelled my eyes to do some exercise. Scanning him as if he were a Skybag in the backscatter X-ray, I devoured the intoxicating aroma of his Nautica Voyage and revelled.

His manly, peppered stubble, his crescent eyebrows (narrow and risen), and his stellar smile that slowly faded into a quizzical frown made some impact on my being. The otherwise confident and composed woman suddenly was seized in a stupor! His gaze met mine and the pang of guilt, probably, played the villain, for he shifted the focus of his eyes to another lovely woman in red. Soon enough, this ethereal encounter evanesced because my client arrived too.

There had been a spark but my mind compelled me to extinguish the incipient flames before they transformed into a conflagration that could destroy both our lives. As the woman in red raised her hands to her cheeks and the man, who had my complete attention, got down on his knees and fished out a ring from his pocket, I realized what a fool I had been in assuming that my flight of fancy could actually turn into a reality. There it was. An early closure to my love tale!

I reminded myself that I was a professional and had a commitment to my client. I forced myself to refocus on my work, pushing aside any thoughts of the mysterious man I had just seen.

"So, what does the prospect of winning this case look like?" asked my client, after silently observing my prolonged divided attention.

"It's complicated. Only if your wife had agreed to do this mutually, things would've been less messier. I'm afraid we'll have to go down the ugly road and build a case that will open a can of worms."

"Any alternate route?" He asked.

"Not really. If you want to have custody of your child, then we'll have to do it. More so because your wife has hired a very experienced and aggressive attorney."

"Hmm, okay."

"We'll see. Let's work on it. The next date is three weeks later. So, we have some time. But you need to …"

I was cut short by a tap on my shoulder. Without expecting anything, I turned only to find the mysteriously handsome man standing right behind me. Flushed red, I tried to hide my uneasiness.

"Hi, I'm Kabir."

"Hi..."

I was speechless. For no particular reason.

"Aren't you Rumi? Rumi, the Whizkid from Army Public School?"

And then it struck me. The floodgates of my memory opened up and I remembered Kabir. The one who always picked on nerds and was mean during my entire time in high school. I hated him, for he made my life miserable. Like how moths are drawn to the street lights, girls used to hover around him even after he was a proven public menace!

"Hey," I began, gathering myself together. The revelation probably contributed to the change of mind; I no longer found him handsome. I no longer fumbled for words.

"I remember you. How have you been? I see you got engaged. Congratulations," I finished in one breath.

"Yes, thanks. She's Sumita. Works in the same office as mine. Anyway, you've changed a lot, Rumi."

"In terms of?"

"In terms of 'not looking like a nerd anymore'. You look lovely," he complimented.

His praise put me in a quandary. My heart fluttered while my mind cautioned. This battle was baffling, for I didn't know which was right. While the glint in his grey eyes signalled some sort of inclination towards me, I couldn't be sure. We chatted for a while and then the connection vanished into the thin air.

The momentary guilt-ridden passion and pleasure that Kabir and I experienced that day were extremely short-lived, for our lives, both personal and professional, seemed more important than the trivial matters of the heart.

Two years passed, and Kabir's life had taken an unexpected turn. His once-happy marriage had crumbled, leaving him and his wife longing for a way out. Seeking a solution, Kabir, aware of my legal prowess, contacted me for a consultation. He had heard of my reputation and believed that I was the one who could help navigate their path to divorce.

I was surprised when I received a call from him, requesting my expertise. I agreed to meet them at the restaurant where our journey had begun. As I entered the familiar establishment, memories flooded back, and I couldn't help but feel a sense of trepidation.

Kabir arrived, looking weary and despondent. His slender fingers pressed upon his temples the moment he sat across from me. And then, the spark that had found home in his eyes years before when we had met in the same restaurant, was back. A slight twinkle in his eyes and he was comfortable enough to pass a genial smile. My heart skipped a beat. I wasn't prepared for this ambush. Two years of absolute 'no contact' had led me to believe that Kabir wasn't the one. He locked eyes with me once again, and this time, the connection between us was undeniable. The circumstances had changed, and we were brought together by a twist of fate. I could see the remorse in Kabir's eyes, the weight of his past actions weighing heavily on him. Or maybe that was my way of convincing my obstinate mind to give 'us' another chance. But that was a far-fetched thought!

During our consultation, I listened attentively to both Kabir and his wife, offering my legal advice and empathetic support. As they spoke, I couldn't help but notice the depth of Kabir's sorrow. For a brief moment, I almost believed his sunken eyes and cursed the almighty for putting him through such misery. But then, as our meetings increased in number, the layers of the facade were peeled off, exposing a profound secret about Kabir's personality that had, all the while, found a safe haven.

He was ignorant. Sumita had her reasons to seek a way out of their communion. Riled up by the slightest provocation, Kabir's inferiority complex had gotten the better of him. Even during our discussions, his modus operandi wasn't that of a mutual filing. He wanted to win. Even if it meant losing someone he once loved.

Fortunately for me, I helped the couple fight their battle in the courtroom and they were granted divorce. But things didn't end there. It's after Sumita (officially) broke all ties with him that he succumbed to a vacuum, a space where he wasn't enough for (even) himself. Constantly questioning his worth and not having anyone by his side to vent out his frustration were the reasons he had received a pink slip. And then, one unfortunate day, he gave me a call.

In a moment of vulnerability, Kabir confessed his feelings to me, admitting that he had been drawn to me from the moment he first laid eyes on me at the restaurant. He expressed his guilt for not having the strength to let go of his crush before, but now, he was convinced that he couldn't live without me.

I listened intently, my heart torn between desire and logic. I admitted to Kabir that I, too, had felt a powerful attraction when we had first met. However, I refused to be with him because I knew him too well. I knew that changing my lifestyle, attitude, and being for someone else would only lead to disappointment and a loss of my true self. I wasn't ready to look for happiness in the wrong places.

As our farewells lingered in the air, Kabir and I embraced the knowledge that our destinies would forever dance in harmony, even if the intricate steps of romance were never fully choreographed. Amidst a tapestry of wistful smiles, we bid adieu, each treading the path of self-discovery and joy, carrying within us the wisdom born of our connection, a treasure of lessons learned, as we embarked on distinct journeys towards our own happiness and contentment.

Gratitude and Appreciation

"Dear Divine Jester above,

Thank you for the cosmic chuckles and divine irony. Your sense of humour keeps life interesting, even when the punchlines are beyond my grasp. Cheers to you for keeping me entertained on this wild ride called existence!"

(But, in all honesty, I really am thankful to you, O Almighty, for giving me the strength and ability to conquer the odds and rise and shine. Again, and again.)

First and foremost, I'd like to extend a warm embrace to my daughter for graciously enduring my late-night editing sessions and persistent typing on the phone. She's been my unwavering source of support, always patient and understanding.

This project has been indirectly fueled by my mother's fondness for romance, inspiring me to transcend practical boundaries and write from the depths of my heart. She's the resilient woman I aspire to become one day. Thank you and love you, mom!

I offer heartfelt thanks to my brother for his candid critique, consistently challenging me to surpass my limits (albeit occasionally testing my patience).

I am deeply grateful to Abhisar, my publisher-cum-friend, whose approachable and amiable demeanor has made collaborating with him an absolute pleasure.

Special gratitude goes to Ms. Sudha Ananth for her adept cover editing and for imparting the basics of layered editing with such patience, which has significantly contributed to the thoughtfully crafted cover.

Last but certainly not least, I express appreciation to AI for assisting me in selecting the perfect images. While it's often a challenge to pinpoint the ideal prompts, the end result consistently radiates beauty. I hope you all take pleasure in immersing yourselves in this heartfelt blend of emotions.

Enjoy Reading.

Enakshi J.

Enakshi J. is a versatile figure, working as an educator, author, and blogger. Her writings have been featured in various publications including The Speaking Tree (Times of India), Woman's Era, Alive, Infinithoughts, SivanaSpirit, Women's Web, EfictionIndia, and Induswomanwriting. Her stories and poems have been included in numerous anthologies. Enakshi has also contributed to a weekly editorial titled Odds and Evens to the social journalism platform Different Truths. She has overseen the conceptualization and editing of three books: *Unbounded Trajectories*, *Poison Ivy*, and *Cryptic Encounters*.

She has authored both *'Star-crossed'* and *'The Green Giants and Other Poems'*. For more information, visit her website at aliveshadow.com.

Instagram: @enakshijohri12